Living Legally

Short Stories Based Upon the Indian Court System

Siva Prasad Bose and Joy Bose

Living Legally: Short Stories Based Upon the Indian Court System

Siva Prasad Bose and Joy Bose

Published by Joy Bose, 2022.

This is a work of fiction. Similarities to real people, places, or events are entirely coincidental.

LIVING LEGALLY: SHORT STORIES BASED UPON THE INDIAN COURT SYSTEM

First edition. November 13, 2022.

Copyright © 2022 Siva Prasad Bose and Joy Bose.

ISBN: 979-8215445624

Written by Siva Prasad Bose and Joy Bose.

Contents

Dedication

<hr>

This book is dedicated to all litigants who are fighting, or have fought, their cases in the Indian courts, sometimes for many years, as well as the judges, lawyers and other participants of the Indian legal system.

Preface

The Indian court system is a large institution. There are thousands of cases being heard daily in the different courts of the land, big and small. Some of the cases run into years and others into decades. It thus affects lakhs or crores of people.

In this book, we write a few stories illustrating different aspects of the Indian court system, how it affects the common people in different situations of life. One of the stories is interpreting the timeless Indian epic, the Mahabharata, as a dispute fought in the Indian courts.

None of these stories are real, any similarity with persons living or dead is purely a matter of coincidence.

Our aim is to present the Indian court system from different viewpoints, and thus help the reader to gain an appreciation of the experience of different aspects of the court system for the common man. At the end of each story, we have added a section on lessons to learn from that story.

The intention is to show how the common man can succeed in getting justice if they persevere, even if the process is slow and fraught with difficulties. It is also worth noting that since this book was first written, India's criminal laws have undergone their most sweeping transformation in over 160 years. From July 2024, three new laws — the Bharatiya Nyaya Sanhita (BNS), the Bharatiya Nagarik Suraksha Sanhita (BNSS), and the Bharatiya

Sakshya Adhiniyam (BSA) — replaced the Indian Penal Code, the Code of Criminal Procedure, and the Indian Evidence Act respectively. The stories and lessons in this book remain as relevant as ever under these new laws, as the fundamental challenges of delay, access to justice, and the experiences of ordinary litigants are largely unchanged.

Acknowledgments

The authors would like to pay their acknowledgements to many friends with whom they held conversations about the Indian court system as well as individual case situations.

We also would like to acknowledge the AI generated art by Midjourney AI and DALL-E 2, which was used for the illustrations in this book.

Chapter 1: Mahabharata as a Court Case

Once there were two brothers named Dhritarashtra and Pandu who lived in a suburb in Delhi called Hastinapur with their parents. Their parents ran a comfortable business and their company was growing and profitable. They also had considerable property and assets.

Dhritarashtra was older than his brother Pandu by a couple of years. However, Dhritarashtra was partly disabled since he was blind from childhood. Therefore, he envied Pandu who was the favourite of their parents. Other than that, both the brothers did not have many problems. They lived in a comfortable upper middle-class home and shared everything they had. They lived as a joint family with aunts and uncles and other relatives in a big villa in a prime location.

When they grew up, both the brothers got married, Dhritarashtra to a girl named Gandhari and Pandu to a girl named Kunti. They soon gave birth to sons, Gandhari to a son named Duryodhana and Kunti to a son named Yudhisthira. Soon after the birth of Yudhisthira, Pandu got diagnosed with cancer and died prematurely. As a result, Dhritarashtra got to manage the family business as the CEO of the company after the death of their parents, with help from the other members of the extended family.

While growing up, at first the cousin brothers Yudhisthira and Duryodhana were friendly to each other and played and studied together and shared all their belongings. But as they grew up, jealousy developed inside Duryodhana towards his cousin brother Yudhisthira. Yudhisthira did well at studies in school while Duryodhana just managed to pass his exams. The same thing happened after school: Yudhisthira got admission in a top-ranking college and a decent job with a multinational corporation (MNC) after graduation. He also married a beautiful girl called Draupadi. Duryodhana just managed to get into a mediocre college and had to struggle for a few years before managing a low paying job. Moreover, his wife Bhanumati was not as good looking and skilled as Yudhisthira's wife Draupadi. Due to all these reasons, Duryodhana developed a lot of negative emotions towards his cousin brother.

After both Yudhisthira and Duryodhana had finished college and got some years of work experience, the time came for the family business to be split between them. Dhritarashtra was currently managing the company as CEO and was naturally partial to his own son Duryodhana. But on the advice of other elders in their joint family, he decided to split the shares 50:50 and hand roughly equal number of divisions of the company to each one.

This arrangement went on for a couple of years, each side managing their part of the business. Through capable strategic leadership and hard work, Yudhisthira was able to efficiently manage and grow his part of the company, while Duryodhana turned out a failure at managing his part of the business. This served only to further increase the jealousy Duryodhana felt towards Yudhisthira.

Aside from the jealousy of not doing as well as Yudhishthira, splitting the company 50:50 in the first place was not acceptable to Duryodhana who used to envy Yudhisthira and wanted full control of the company for himself. He felt that was his right in lieu of his father Dhritarashtra being the CEO of the business. So, with the help of his maternal uncle, Shakuni, he hatched upon a cunning plan.

Despite being blessed with many virtues and skills, Yudhisthira had one bad habit, in that he liked to gamble. Taking advantage of his weakness, Duryodhana and Shakuni challenged him to a game of dice whose terms were codified in a contract signed by both parties in the presence of witnesses.

As per the terms, if either party lost in the game of dice, he and his wife would have to go abroad for 12 years, and their business assets would be managed by the other party in their absence. On returning to India after 12 years, they would get back their share of 50% of the company and things would go back to the way they were earlier.

Yudhisthira fell for the bait and got defeated by Shakuni, who was the regional champion at gambling. Consequently, he had to go abroad as agreed and the 50% of the company was taken away by Duryodhana. As per the contract, Yudhishthira and his wife left India for 12 years and spent a few years in Europe as the export sales manager for the MNC where he was working.

Yudhishthira skilfully utilized his time abroad for upgrading his business skills and making new contacts through networking, while Duryodhana tried to cement his hold on the company with the help of a coterie of close advisors.

Figure: Two persons playing a game of dice in India. AI generated art by Midjourney AI

After 12 years were over, Yudhisthira and his wife Draupadi sought to return to India, and Yudhisthira sent his wise friend and cousin Krishna to negotiate with Duryodhana for getting back 50% of the company. When Krishna arrived in Hastinapur to discuss terms, Duryodhana flatly refused to share any part of the business with his cousin brother as per the original contract. The elders of the joint family also tried to reason with Duryodhana, but to no avail.

Having no other option, Yudhisthira decided to file a court case against Duryodhana for getting control of his rightful part of the company, as per the original terms of the contract. The case was filed in Kurukshetra district court. Duryodhana, who was managing the business while Yudhisthira was abroad, by now had carefully cultivated an army of lawyers to fight the case on his behalf, while Yudhisthira mainly had his friend Krishna as his advisor.

Soon the court hearings started. Duryodhana's lawyers tried to make their case on the basis of forged documents showing that the company ownership was supposed to be his and the contract was void, while Yudhishthira's lawyers pleaded the court for enforcement of the original contract. Both the sides presented evidence and witnesses to support their case, however while Yudhishthira's witnesses and documents were genuine, those of Duryodhana's were forged and the witnesses coerced.

Figure: Scene in an Indian court. AI generated art by Midjourney AI

The Indian court system typically moves slowly. The process of presenting of arguments and hearings took a number of years. Since Yudhishthira's case had a stronger legal foundation, his case was stronger even though Duryodhana had hired many expensive lawyers. Eventually Yudhisthira won the case in the lower court, which ruled that the original contract was valid. But promptly Duryodhana appealed the verdict in higher courts. The case thus went on for 18 years, with each time Duryodhana losing and his lawyers appealing to a higher court. Duryodhana had to change his lawyers several times, since they kept losing in their arguments before the honourable judges.

While the case was going on, in the meantime Duryodhana also tried a few dirty tricks to intimidate Yudhishthira's side. These included tactics such as giving threats to Yudhishthira's family, defamatory articles posted in the local media with the help of paid journalists, creating obstructions for the electricity and water supply of the house where Yudhishthira was staying by bribing some municipal employees, and so on.

Many a times, because of all these tactics, Yudhisthira felt like giving up the court case and settling it, but his wise friend Krishna advised him to fight in search of justice without getting greedy or being attached to the eventual outcome of the court case. Because of this wise advice, Yudhishthira got the strength to fight on.

Figure: Cross examination of witnesses in an Indian court. AI generated art by Midjourney AI

Eventually the appeals for the case reached the Supreme Court of India. Yudhishthira's lawyers were able to conclusively establish that Duryodhana's documents were forged, and their contract was legally enforceable. As a result, here too Duryodhana lost the appeal.

For all the years the court case was going on, Yudhishthira managed his own career well and kept working for the multinational company, where he kept getting salary increments and promotions due to his hard work. On the other hand, Duryodhana in his greed for control of the company made the mistake of focusing entirely on the court case and consequently was not able to increase his income or assets. His management of the company was also going poorly.

Consequently, once Duryodhana lost the court case, he had lost everything: he had few assets and his career was in shambles. In contrast, Yudhishthira now had a good position and a good job as well as winning the case. Thinking about this made Duryodhana mad with frustration. His mental health took a toll.

In his desperation, a few days later Duryodhana and a couple of acolytes crept into the premises of the company during the night and set fire to it. A lot of the assets of the company were damaged as a result. Yudhishthira lodged a police complaint and eventually Duryodhana was caught and jailed by the police.

Yudhishthira had managed to win the case after a long period of 18 years, but the company was in shambles due to mismanagement by Duryodhana and its assets burnt down. With great hard work and business skills gained over the years, Yudhishthira managed to rebuild the company back to prosperity and growth as its new CEO. The company went back to profitability and Yudhishthira was able to expand the business in various sectors and even overseas.

Figure: Yudhishthira presiding over a board meeting of the company as CEO. AI generated art by Midjourney AI

Instead of enjoying a comfortable life as a co-owner of the business, Duryodhana because of his jealousy and deceit was financially ruined had now to spend his years in jail.

Lesson from the story:

The Indian legal system can sometimes be slow in delivering justice. Sometimes cases take years or even decades in delivering a verdict, on top of it the execution and appeals process can take even longer. To fight and win such cases, one needs skills of perseverance, good time management, and a good plan. One also needs good friends one can turn to in times of trouble. It is important not to neglect one's own career when fighting the court cases. Also, one needs to pay attention to their physical and mental well-being. Being greedy for quick results and trying illegal actions does not pay in the long run, for the court system does manage to deliver justice to those who are hardworking and persistently fight their court cases against all odds.

Chapter 2: Tale of the Stressed Judge

Vidyabhushan, one of the judges in a District Court, was a very busy man. He had a lot of cases pending before him. His superiors wanted him to close many of the cases by the end of the year, in order to improve their rate of disposal of cases. This was putting pressure on him.

Moreover, some of the cases involved politically influential people who were also starting to subtly put pressure on him to give a verdict in a certain way. There were constant media trials and social media scrutiny of court judgments. Vidyabhushan also had to manage his career to get timely promotions and keep up to date with the latest important judgements from the higher courts.

As a result of all this, Vidyabhushan had less time for personal life. Coming to court in the morning, sitting in the court all day, hearing arguments, giving judgments and hearing appeals were all physically exhausting for him.

Figure: Judge sitting in an Indian court. AI generated art by Midjourney AI

Often, Vidyabhushan had to take the case files home after work to read them before the next day's hearing. Also, he had to take care of his own family. When he went back home after a busy day at court, he had very less energy to tutor his daughter, who was giving her high school exams in a few months.

All the stress eventually took a toll on Vidyabhushan's health. He developed stress related sicknesses such as diabetes and had trouble sleeping and an erratic heartbeat. He also began to be depressed sometimes. Soon, he had to miss case hearings multiple times due to ill health, which then affected his chances of promotion and led to further stress.

Eventually Vidyabhushan had to resign from his job in order to protect his mental and physical health from further damage. He then took a lighter job adjudicating disputes which was less stressful than that of a full-time judge, but which also paid less.

Lesson from the story:

Judges in India have a high standing in society, yet their job too can be stressful. The huge caseloads and lack of sufficient new judge recruitments in the Indian legal system makes the life of existing judges more difficult. Litigants often do not appreciate the work involved and the mental stress of being a judge in Indian courts.

Chapter 3: Story of the Poor Undertrial

Manish used to run a small tea shop on the outskirts of a small town in India. He had been running the shop since his childhood, when he used to help his father who ran the shop before him. Over the years, he had become an expert in making masala chai and serving it in the kulhad or mud cup. He has a small but dedicated regular clientele, who came to his shop every morning and evening to have tea and chit chat about life. His earnings, though low, were stable and just enough to take care of his small family and son's education in a local school.

One day, disaster struck. Arun, a local mafia boss, who was thinking of joining a big political party, came and demanded that Manish sell his shop to him at a very cheap rate. Arun needed the land to build a shopping mall and get lots of money from potential buyers, that would potentially fund his election campaign once he joined the party. Since the tea shop was the only source of his livelihood, Manish did not agree. He pleaded with Arun to spare him and his tea shop, but to no avail.

Soon after, one morning the police came and arrested Manish from his home. Arun had bribed Manish's neighbour who falsely accused Manish of stealing his bicycle. Using his influence on the local police office, he got the police to arrest Manish without a proper investigation and put him in jail as an undertrial. His family were devastated since Manish was the sole breadwinner of the family. Manish was put in a tiny cell along with 10 other people, all of whom were poor undertrials and similarly accused of various petty crimes. His family, after a lot of difficulty and after using up most of his tiny savings, managed to hire a lawyer to defend Manish.

Soon after, once Manish was locked up in jail for a week, the local municipal corporation officers came and demolished his teashop, claiming it was an illegal construction on government land. This was even though Manish had been regularly paying his taxes and running the shop for many decades, after his father who also used to do the same.

Figure: Scene in a dirty Indian jail with a group of undertrials. AI generated art by DALL-E 2

Life in jail was tough for Manish. The conditions in the jail cell were unsanitary. The food of cold rice and water-diluted lentils was stale and sometimes had dead insects in it. He had to sleep on the cold floor, and there was no protection from mosquitoes. Occasional visits from his wife and family were the only thing he had to look forward to. But Manish still had hope that one day he would be proven innocent and able to start the tea shop again.

Figure: A courtroom scene with a group of undertrials in an Indian court. AI generated art by DALL-E 2

The days soon passed to months. His case dragged on in the local court. Manish's lawyer often missed the court dates. The judge was sometimes absent, and the court dates kept getting shifted. Soon two years were gone, and there was no progress in the case. Manish feared he would have to spend the rest of his life in jail.

One day, Manish received a visit from members of an NGO (non-governmental organization) comprising of activist lawyers working to free undertrials, and who offered to fight his case for free. They had gone through the details in his case and felt there was a chance of getting him released. Soon, the new lawyers made afresh appeal, and pointed to contradictions in the case of the prosecution. The judge was forced to admit the case lacked merit, and ordered the police to free Manish.

Finally, one day Manish walked out of jail a free man. Justice had been done. However, by then it was too late. His tea shop was gone, his son had to drop out from school, and his wife had to work as a domestic servant to make ends meet. In place of the tea shop was now a huge mall, built by Arun who had recently won the local elections and became a corporator.

Manish had neither the energy nor the resources to fight Arun in the courts. So he decided to negotiate. After a lot of pleading, Arun gave him a part time job as a security guard at the mall built over his tea shop. Things were bad, but at least Manish could again focus on re-building his life.

Lesson from the story:

Thousands of undertrials in India such as Manish are trapped in jail for years on end. They have neither been proved guilty nor innocent, and their cases are dragging on in the courts while their lives are put on hold. Richer people may have access to better lawyers to fight their cases, but the poor do not. As of 2025, undertrials account for approximately 76% of India's total prison population — nearly 4.4 lakh people — and Indian prisons operate at over 130% of their intended capacity. Recognizing this crisis, Parliament enacted the Bharatiya Nagarik Suraksha Sanhita (BNSS), 2023, which came into force in July 2024. Section 479 of the BNSS now requires first-time offenders to be released on bail once they have served one-third of the maximum sentence for their alleged offence, and other undertrials after serving half. The Supreme Court has directed these provisions apply retrospectively to eligible prisoners. Yet the pace of implementation remains slow, and poor people like Manish continue to be the most unfortunate victims of a system in urgent need of reform.

The courts system in India is very slow moving, and poor people like Manish are the most unfortunate victims.

Chapter 4: Tale of the Lazy Son and the Will

———

Once there was a rich farmer who owned some lands in a village in Karnataka state of India.

He had two sons. The elder son was industrious and hardworking while the younger one was lazy and greedy. To earn extra money and support his family, the elder son went to work in a city where he established a small business and was able to earn and save more money than if he had just stayed in the village. The younger son, being lazy, just stayed and helped to cultivate his father's lands, hoping secretly that his father will leave him all the lands after his death. However, the farmer father loved both sons equally and did not show any partiality towards any son.

After some years, the farmer died. Before dying, he wrote a will and divided his lands equally between the two sons. The elder son was quite happy with this, but the younger was not, since he wanted to occupy the whole land and felt that the fact he had stayed with his father entitled him to get the complete land. Therefore, he felt that it was his right to occupy the whole of it rather than give away half to his elder brother who lived in the city and only occasionally came to the village to visit.

Additionally, since he was living with his father and taking care of his fields, he already had the advantage of possession of the property and vowed never to give it up, regardless of what his father wished, or his elder brother would do.

To get the whole land, the younger son managed to forge a copy of the will by forging his father's signature. In the forged will, the entire land was given to him and none to the elder son. In this way, there were two versions of the farmers' will, in one version both the sons were getting an equal share and in the other all of it was going to one son and none to the other. Additionally, the younger son succeeded in registering his forged copy of the will with the local registry office in the tehsil by paying bribes to the local registrar.

When the elder son went to court to enforce the original will of his father, the younger one opposed it saying that his forged copy, that gave the entire land to him, was the real version. Soon the case ended up in court.

Figure: A busy court scene in India. AI generated art by Midjourney AI

Like in most lower court cases involving property disputes, the case dragged on for years. It was a painful task to go to the capital of the district to attend the court hearings. Many times, the hearings were adjourned and the judge was transferred and the new judge took additional time to hear the case.

The younger son also tried various cunning tactics such as filing new cases on petty pretexts, just to further delay the case and enjoy his possession of the father's land for longer while the case dragged on and on. He also bribed some local witnesses to give false testimonies of his father's wishes before he died, to build the case that his version of the will was true.

In this way the case went on for more than 10 years. The elder brother almost wanted to give up the case, considering how much effort he had to go through to hire a lawyer, pay the lawyers fees, travel to the district court on the court date and so on. Yet, for the interest of justice, he felt like fighting on. He was certainly earning more money from his business in the town than his brother was, even though his brother had the advantage of possession of the property and local witnesses whom he could bribe.

After many years, the case finally case to the final stage of evidence. Despite all kinds of tactics and threats by the younger son, the elder son's lawyer managed to get the court to agree on a forensic scan of the two wills from the government laboratory, to establish which will was genuine and which was forged. As a result, he was able to show that his younger brother's will was the forged one. He thus managed to win the case and justice was served. The court ruled that as per the genuine will, the father's land should be equally divided between his two sons.

Even after winning the case, the elder son's problems were not over. Since the younger son still had possession and refused to hand over the elder son's share of the land, he again had to apply for execution of the judgment, which took some more time but eventually succeeded. The younger son, to further delay the case, contemplated an appeal in the higher courts, but eventually gave up once he found out the cost of such an appeal. So, after all these years, the elder son finally got his just inheritance.

Lesson from the story:

Property disputes, concerning wills and property sharing, often within members of the same extended family, sometimes take many years or even decades to get justice in the courts. One should not let this unfortunate fact make them lose faith in justice. By fighting a resolute battle and not being scared or expecting quick justice, but by perseverance, justice will be delivered in the courts. Justice may be late sometimes but is never lost.

Chapter 5: Story of the Bad Neighbour

There was an old couple, Mr. and Mrs. Tripathi, who lived alone in a house in a big city. They had a son, but he was living with his family in a distant city and only occasionally came to visit them. Now, the house of Mr. Tripathi was located in a posh locality, and could fetch a very good price when sold. So, it caught the eye of a cunning neighbour named Mr. Balwant who was living in a nearby house in the same locality.

Figure: Old couple living in a house in India. AI generated art by Midjourney AI

Balwant thought, what if I could just make life so unbearable for the old couple, that they would be forced to sell or leave their house and then I could get it for free or for a very low price. Thus thinking, he developed a plan to harass and drive away the Tripathi couple. Balwant's scheming wife also helped him to refine the plan and make it fool-proof.

Soon after, Mr. and Mrs. Tripathi went to visit their son and daughter in law for a month. But on returning to their home after one month, the couple started having a number of daily problems. Their electricity bill became unbearably high, so did their water bill, the water got cut at random hours, their mailbox was broken and newspapers and mail in the mailbox started getting stolen, their daily domestic workers started getting threats, there was garbage on their front lawn and so on.

Unknown to the Tripathi couple, when they were gone the cunning neighbour Balwant had some wires installed to steal their electricity and employed a plumber to install extra pipes and taps to divert their municipal water supply and control it. He also started tactics such as threatening the domestic help of the old couple, breaking the mailbox and stealing stuff from it and leaving garbage about. Such incidents of harassment gradually increased month by month.

Eventually the Tripathis came to know who was responsible and went to Balwant's house to complain, but Balwant refused to stop and further threatened them instead. This led to an argument and Balwant pushed Mr. Tripathi, who fell to the ground and hurt himself.

Figure: Old man in an argument with a neighbour. AI generated art by Midjourney AI

Initially, Mr. Tripathi did not report the incidents to the police since he was afraid of the police and unfamiliar with their procedures, being old and frail. But as the harassment incidents from Balwant became more and more frequent, Mr. Tripathi was left with no option and had to approach the local police in the city to file a complaint.

But the police were, as is often the case in India, reluctant to register an FIR in order to avoid extra work and improve their statistics of lodged FIRs. They demanded proofs such as video evidence which Mr. Tripathi was unable to collect, being aged and unfamiliar with technology. As a result, the police took no concrete action but only promised the Tripathi couple to send a beat policeman once every other month to check on their safety.

Finally, the Tripathi couple became desperate and with the help of their son and some local friends, hired a lawyer to get the courts to come to their aid. The lawyer sent a legal notice to Balwant to stop the harassment actions, and also filed a case in the civil court to force the police to file an FIR and investigate the ongoing complaints. They also made a complaint with the SDM of the district under the Senior Citizens Protection Act.

Eventually, with the commencement of the legal case, the local police were forced to register a case. Soon, the police came to Mr. Balwant's house to interview him, with which Balwant got a little scared. The incidents of threats and other harassment by Balwant soon stopped. Mrs. Tripathi got a few people to fix their water and electricity supply. Balwant's plan to drive away the couple by harassing them and get their house cheaply thus got foiled.

Lesson from the story:

Sometimes, the senior citizens are seen as soft targets by unscrupulous people eyeing their property. The law has some safeguards for the protection of senior citizens from abuse and such safeguards can be utilized skilfully. It is important for senior citizens and their well wishers to keep abreast of existing laws and mechanisms for their protection and utilize them as needed.

Chapter 6: Tale of the Vengeful Wife

Once there was a man named Amit who was working as a software engineer in a company in a big city. Like most software engineers, he had to work long hours and was still always afraid of getting fired. However, his salary was decent even though he did not get too many increments or promotions. He even managed to save enough money for buying a small apartment, with the help of bank loans.

Eventually his parents pressurized him to get married. His wife Sunita was from a small town and was unfamiliar with IT lifestyle of long working hours and stressful jobs with no job security. Sunita's father was a police officer in their town. Soon after the marriage, Sunita moved to live in the city with her new husband Amit.

Figure: Indian wedding scene. AI generated art by Midjourney AI

Initially their marriage was going well and both had a happy life. However, it soon became apparent there was a mismatch of expectations. The wife Sunita was expecting a life of comfort with the husband Amit's salary. She was not used to the pressures of living in a big city and having to deal with Amit's long working hours and the insecure nature of his IT job.

This mismatch of expectations led to domestic fights between Amit and Sunita only a few months into their marriage. The fights soon increased in intensity and frequency. The neighbours too got concerned about the brawls that were often in late hours after Amit returned from his office.

Figure: Argument between husband and wife in India. AI generated art by Midjourney AI

One day Amit and Sunita had a huge fight and Sunita left for her mother's place in a huff. There, she spoke to friends and found out about the wife friendly laws such as 498a (anti dowry act) and DV (prevention of domestic violence act) which did not need much proof aside of allegations, and which she could use to blackmail her husband for a huge amount of money.

Sunita also found a greedy lawyer who was all too happy to help her write the false allegations that are needed for 498a and DV, even though Amit's family had never really pressurized her for dowry. The lawyer only wanted 10% of the final settlement from the husband Amit after the case was won, which he was confident he would be able to get at least 1 crore as the settlement amount.

Sunita and her lawyer went to a mahila thana (women's police station) in their town and filed the complaint for 498a and domestic violence, naming the husband Amit and all his family members including Amit's old mother and father and even Amit's sister as accomplices.

Soon after, Amit received a call from the local police inspector informing him that an FIR had been lodged on behalf of his wife, and asking him to come to the police station to join the investigation.

Amit was pretty shocked on getting the call from the police, for he had no idea that his wife Sunita would go to this extent due to just some domestic fights. When he went to the police station, the police threatened to arrest him and openly asked for Rs 20000 as bribe to remove the names of his parents and sister from the FIR, and Amit felt he had no choice but to pay the same.

Figure: Cross examination scene in an Indian court. AI generated art by Midjourney AI

Soon the court dates started, which were in Sunita's hometown. To fight the case, Amit had to hire a local lawyer in his wife's hometown, take leaves from his work and attend each of the court dates. The local lawyer, however, turned out to be unreliable and more interested in milking Amit for his money than in actually fighting the case. All this caused a lot of stress to Amit and impacted his work performance, which led to him being fired from his job. With great difficulty he was able to find another, slightly lower paying, IT job in a different company.

Being desperate, Amit managed to find a group of people in his city who were trapped in similar kinds of cases and could support each other. With their help, he managed to get a more decent lawyer and formulate a strategy to fight the false cases.

Figure: Lawyer arguing a case in an Indian court. AI generated art by Midjourney AI

The 498 and DV cases dragged on for a few years. By now Amit had gotten experienced in how these things worked and how best to collect the evidence to disprove the false allegations of his wife Sunita. Eventually, the court found him not guilty.

Being left with no options, Sunita's side then came forward to compromise and they were able to jointly file for a Section 13B mutual consent divorce petition, which got approved in its due time. Finally, Amit was able to break free from the stress of the court cases and remarry.

But alas, all these years of running around the courts had stunted Amit's career growth and wages, and also had a toll on his father who had passed away in the midst of the case. Despite this, Amit had now found a new confidence to handle any and all court cases that might come his way and his determination, hard work and support from the well wishers had finally paid off.

Lesson from the story:

Some laws in India are easy to be misused by unscrupulous people, and this can cause a lot of suffering for the affected persons and their families. The way out is to be determined and persistent in the cause of justice and not to be swayed by threats of police etc. It is relevant to note that from July 2024, IPC Section 498A (cruelty by a husband or his relatives) has been re-enacted as Section 84 of the new Bharatiya Nyaya Sanhita (BNS), 2023, retaining the same essential provisions. The new laws also strengthen forensic investigation requirements and introduce mandatory videography for certain procedures, which over time may help reduce the misuse of such provisions while continuing to protect genuine victims.

If a person is persistent and ready to fight, despite all the drawbacks of the implementation of the laws, they will eventually win justice in the Indian courts.

Therefore, in the face of false cases and setbacks, one should never get depressed or distressed, but fight on with determination.

Chapter 7: Tale of the Greedy Lawyer

Once there was a big and famous senior lawyer named Sudarshan who lived in a medium sized town in India. Even though it was not a big city, it had plenty of cases of all kinds: property disputes, criminal cases, family disputes, matrimonial cases and so on. As a result of hard work, Sudarshan became famous in the town and even all over the state. People came from far away to request him to take their case. He started charging unusually high fees and still the people were ready to pay whatever he asked.

Figure: Lawyer arguing a case in an Indian court. AI generated art by Midjourney AI

When he was a junior lawyer, Sudarshan used to be careful and ethical about which cases to take and which not to. He would not take on cases unless he was himself convinced of his client being in the right. However, as he became big and famous, Sudarshan stopped evaluating cases and took on any case where the client could afford his fees.

Once Sudarshan was approached by rich client regarding a new case. The client was a businessman and wanted his help in a fraud case. As was now his standard practice, Sudarshan took on the case without much analysis, simply because the client agreed to pay him a huge bonus on top of his regular fees.

Later, after a few hearings had passed, Sudarshan felt that the client's case was weak as per the law and the opposite party's case was strong. To keep his record unblemished, he wanted desperately to get off the case. Moreover, more than half of his fees had already been paid by the client by then.

All Sudarshan wanted was some plausible pretext to leave the case. With this in mind, Sudarshan started missing to appear on some of the case dates. Also, while the first case hearings were going on, the opposite party brought a perjury case on Sudarshan's client. Instead of fighting the new case as well, Sudarshan took the opportunity to tell the client that this new case was not agreed in advance, he had no time from the existing case load and therefore the client needed to hire a new lawyer for the same.

The client had no choice but to engage a new lawyer for the ongoing case as well as the new case. However, when he came to Sudarshan to collect his case documents, Sudarshan demanded an additional hefty sum of money failing which he would keep the client's case files and not give a no objection certificate.

The client was by then quite angry at Sudarshan's refusal to cooperate, his frequent absences and now his refusal to release his documents without taking an additional hefty amount. So, he complained to the bar council about Sudarshan's conduct and sought the help of the bar council to get Sudarshan to release his case documents.

The bar council, after a couple of hearings, then ordered Sudarshan to release the case files to the client. Sudarshan had no choice but to do the same. Moreover, his client, who was a moderately influential person in the town, spread the word around about Sudarshan's conduct regarding his case.

As a result, Sudarshan's clients slowly started to decrease. Soon, Sudarshan was struggling to get enough new clients who could afford his fees. He started to reflect what had gone wrong, from being the top lawyer in demand in the city and probably even the state to the place where he was now, with not enough clients hiring him. He realized that in his greed for money, he had unwittingly ended up sacrificing his professionalism, and this had hurt his promising career.

Lesson from the story:

While most of the lawyers may be honest and hardworking, sometimes one may get a lawyer who is unscrupulous and cares more about the client's money than about fighting the case.

In such cases, the clients should not be afraid to demand professional conduct from their lawyer and failing the same not be afraid to change their lawyer for a better one.

Clients in Indian court cases need to cultivate the skills to hire principled and hardworking lawyers, manage their lawyers properly and fight the case together.

Chapter 8: Story of the First Day

"How dare they try to take my property from me!"

Thoughts raged in Ravi's mind. For today was the date his court case was going to start. The case he had been waiting for the last three years. The case which would bring back his self-esteem, finally redeeming it from years of humiliation, by his own siblings no less.

"What didn't I do for my brothers, and this is how they repay me!"

"Today I will show them all what a court case is really like!"

But Ravi also had a few thoughts full of doubt. "But what if my lawyer doesn't turn up, after charging me so much money? Or worse, what if he is allied to the opposite party and taken money from them?"

Raging with thoughts of anger, confusion, fear and a myriad of other emotions, Ravi called his lawyer. "Awasthi Sir, are you coming to the court? I am already driving there! We must not be late!"

The lawyer tried to calm him down "Don't worry Mr. Ravi, I am only stuck in a bit of traffic jam. Anyway, I have asked my subordinate to be there and he has almost reached the court premises." Eventually, the lawyer arrived, and Ravi reached the court with his lawyer but after a delay of 20 minutes.

After a security check and with some effort, Ravi and his lawyer located the right courtroom where their case hearing was fixed. Their hearing was listed at number 6 in the day's schedule. So, they went to the courtroom and waited. Their opposite party and their lawyer were also present.

However, 30 minutes had passed since the courtroom opened, it was full of people and only the judge was missing. Ravi waited and waited, with great anticipation and full of expectations as to what might happen.

Figure: A busy court hearing in India. AI generated art by Midjourney AI

After 35 minutes, the clerk announced that the judge was on leave and therefore won't be coming that day. They announced the next hearing date which was 2 months away. On hearing this, Ravi got a huge shock. All his expectations were in the mud. He almost fainted, but then managed to compose himself.

Soon the days became months, months became years and the court hearings continued at a snail's pace. Ravi finally understood that he would have to be patient to get his much-anticipated revenge. Very, very patient.

Lesson from the story:

This story illustrates the futility of expecting a quick justice from the Indian courts. Even though some people may feel they are in the right, the court system can be sometimes slow and it can take years or even decades for justice to be delivered.

The qualities of hard work, thorough case building, effective time management and persistence are invaluable qualities for any litigant fighting cases in Indian courts.

Chapter 9: Tale of the Landlord

Mr. Venkappa was a landlord in Bangalore for many years. He owned several apartments in Bangalore in areas like Koramangala and Indiranagar. From the rental income, he lived out his retirement days comfortably with his wife. His son and daughter in law were settled and working in the US.

Figure: An old landlord in Bangalore in South India collecting rent from a tenant. AI generated art by DALL-E 2

However, Mr. Venkappa's life took a drastic turn one day. One of his tenants, Mr. Srihari, filed a false case against him in the district court, claiming that Mr. Venkappa had evicted him without giving proper notice and without giving back his 10 months security deposit. Mr. Venkappa was shocked when he got the summons from the court saying a case had been filed against him and he had to appear in the court on the next date, failing which proceedings will be decided ex-parte. He considered himself a law-abiding citizen, and never thought he would have to go round the courts in his old age.

With great difficulty, Mr. Venkappa was able to hurriedly appoint a lawyer to represent him in the court. His son, being in the US, was unable to help. The case eventually went to trial. Mr. Venkappa's health worsened with all the additional stress of the court case and handling the lawyers.

However, the case did not go well for Mr. Venkappa. Mr. Srihari's lawyers presented false evidence which Mr. Venkappa's lawyer was unable to refute effectively. The judge did not listen to Mr. Venkappa's side of the story. Eventually, the verdict went against Mr Venkappa, and he was ordered to pay a large sum of money to Mr. Srihari with interest as compensation.

Unable to bear the defeat, and despite the additional stress, Mr. Venkappa with the help of some friends began to independently reinvestigate the case and the opposite party evidence in detail. He talked to other witnesses and gathered evidence that showed Mr. Srihari's claims were false. He also discovered that Mr. Srihari had a history of filing false cases against other landlords.

Armed with this new evidence, Mr. Venkappa with the help of his lawyer filed an appeal in the Karnataka High Court. The High Court took note of the new evidence and ordered a retrial. This time, Mr. Venkappa's lawyer was able to present the evidence that showed Mr. Srihari's claims were false. The judge finally ruled in Mr. Venkappa's favour, and the false case against him was dismissed.

Thus, after a lot of struggle and stress, Mr. Venkappa could fend off the false case and finally get justice in the court. However, the huge amount of time and energy pursuing the case, and the lawyer's high fees, cost him quite a bit in terms of time and money and ruined his dream of a peaceful time after retirement.

Lesson from the story:

This story shows that justice in India, though not easy or quick, can eventually come to one who is persistent in their quest for justice. It also highlights that fact that landlords and many other ordinary people from all walks of life can sometimes fall under the trap of false cases filed by greedy and unscrupulous people.

Chapter 10: Tale of the Digital Fraud

Ramakrishnan Pillai was a retired bank manager who lived with his wife in a quiet colony in Thiruvananthapuram. Having spent thirty-five years in a nationalized bank, he understood money and accounts better than most. After retirement, he managed the family's modest savings carefully, moving some into fixed deposits and a little into mutual funds on the advice of his son, who worked in Bengaluru as a software engineer.

One morning, Ramakrishnan received a phone call from a man who introduced himself as an officer from TRAI, the Telecom Regulatory Authority of India. The caller spoke in a formal, authoritative tone and informed Ramakrishnan that his mobile number had been flagged for suspicious activity and would be disconnected within two hours unless he cooperated with a verification process. Ramakrishnan, alarmed at the prospect of losing his number, agreed to cooperate.

The caller then transferred the call to a second person who claimed to be a senior police officer from the Delhi Cyber Crime Branch. This man told Ramakrishnan, in a grave voice, that his Aadhaar number had been used to open a bank account in Mumbai, and that account had been used to launder money. He was told that he was under "digital arrest" — a term the caller used confidently — and must not leave his home or speak to anyone, including his family, until the investigation was cleared. To prove his innocence, he would have to transfer his savings temporarily to a "government escrow account" for verification.

Terrified and confused, Ramakrishnan asked no questions. He was a law-abiding man who had never once had a dispute with any authority. The idea that he could be accused of money laundering was incomprehensible to him. Over the next two days, under instructions from the callers who remained connected by video call almost continuously, he transferred Rs 18 lakh in several instalments to different bank accounts. After the final transfer, the callers abruptly disconnected and stopped responding. Ramakrishnan sat in stunned silence in his drawing room, slowly understanding what had happened.

His son Arun, calling from Bengaluru that evening, immediately grasped the situation. He asked his father to note down all the account numbers and call records and drove overnight to Thiruvananthapuram. Together, they went to the nearest police station the next morning to file a complaint. The duty officer, however, was unfamiliar with cyber fraud procedures and initially asked them to come back the next day. Arun firmly insisted on filing a complaint immediately. He had read about the national helpline for cyber fraud — the number 1930 — and had already called it the previous night to report the fraud and freeze the destination accounts.

An FIR was eventually registered under the Bharatiya Nyaya Sanhita, 2023, which came into force in July 2024 and contains specific provisions addressing financial fraud, cheating by impersonation, and organised cybercrime — offences that had previously been handled in a more fragmented manner under the old Indian Penal Code and the Information Technology Act. The new laws also treat electronic evidence — call records, screen recordings, and bank transaction logs — as primary evidence on an equal footing with physical documents.

The Kerala Cyber Crime Cell took up the case and traced two of the recipient accounts to an organised network operating from a different state. Through coordination with the banking authorities, approximately Rs 4 lakh was frozen before it could be moved further, and was eventually returned to Ramakrishnan. The remaining Rs 14 lakh had been quickly layered through multiple accounts and withdrawn as cash — a common tactic to make recovery impossible.

The criminal case dragged on for several years. No arrests were made in the first year, and the investigators admitted that the masterminds of such organised networks were often difficult to trace. Arun hired a cyber law advocate to monitor the progress of the case and file periodic applications before the court for updates on the investigation. The court, under the new procedural framework of the BNSS, could direct the police to submit status reports at fixed intervals, which provided some accountability where earlier there had been none.

For Ramakrishnan, the loss of Rs 14 lakh was devastating. It represented years of careful savings. His wife, who had been kept in the dark during the two days of calls, wept when she finally learnt the full story. The couple had to significantly reduce their living expenses and depend more on their son. Ramakrishnan could not sleep properly for months, tormented by the thought that despite his years in banking, he had been deceived so completely.

Gradually, however, his son Arun encouraged him to channel his experience into something useful. Ramakrishnan began visiting the local senior citizens' association and schools to speak about digital fraud. He explained, in simple terms, how "digital arrest" was a fiction with no basis in Indian law — no court or police authority can place a citizen under such a thing through a phone call. He described the tactics the fraudsters had used and how to identify them. Slowly, word spread and he became known in his neighbourhood as a person to consult about cyber safety. The experience, though deeply painful, had given him a mission.

Lesson from the story:

Cyber fraud, and in particular the "digital arrest" scam, has become one of the most widespread forms of crime affecting ordinary Indians in recent years. Victims have included retired professionals, government employees, doctors, teachers, and even lawyers. No educational background provides immunity; the fraudsters are skilled at creating panic and bypassing rational thought.

The key points to remember are these. First, there is no such thing as "digital arrest" in Indian law. No police officer, court, or government agency will demand money over the telephone or insist that a citizen remain isolated at home under a video call. Second, if one receives such a call, the right response is to immediately disconnect, verify the caller's claims independently by contacting the official numbers of TRAI or the police, and report the call to the national cyber fraud helpline on 1930 or at cybercrime.gov.in. Third, speed is essential. The faster a complaint is filed, the greater the chance that the fraudsters' bank accounts can be frozen before the money is withdrawn.

India's new Bharatiya Nyaya Sanhita, 2023 and Bharatiya Sakshya Adhiniyam, 2023 have strengthened the legal framework for prosecuting cybercriminals and allow electronic evidence to be used directly in court proceedings. However, the law can only help those who report crimes promptly. One must speak to family members immediately if approached by such callers, for a single calm voice from someone one trusts is often enough to break the trance of fear that these fraudsters so expertly create.

About the Authors

Siva Prasad Bose is a writer of introductory guidebooks on different aspects of Indian laws. He is also a retired electrical engineer, retired after many years of service in Uttar Pradesh Power Corporation Limited. He received his engineering degree from Jadavpur University, Kolkata and has a law degree from Meerut University, Meerut and a Bachelor of Science from MMH University Ghaziabad. His interests lie in the fields of family law, civil law, law of contracts, and areas of law related to power electricity related issues.

Joy Bose is a researcher, data scientist, and co-author of multiple books on Indian law and society. He holds a Master of Laws (LLM) from Golden Gate University, San Francisco.

Other books by Siva Prasad Bose

———

Introduction to Wills and Probate

Delays in Court Cases in India

Introduction to Negotiable Instruments

Introduction to Marriage Laws in India

Neighbor Problems in India and what to do about them

Managing Court Cases with Mental Strength

Introduction to Patents and Patent Law in India

Introduction to Property Law in India

Did you love *Living Legally: Short Stories Based Upon the Indian Court System*? Then you should read *Introduction to Street Law in India*[1] by Siva Prasad Bose!

[2]

Introduction to Street Law in India

A Practical Guide to Everyday Legal Problems

Every day, millions of Indians face legal situations they don't know how to handle: a noisy neighbor, an unfair dismissal, an online scam, a disputed inheritance. The law protects you in all of these situations. But only if you know it.

---

1. https://books2read.com/u/mgjWX7

2. https://books2read.com/u/mgjWX7

Street Law in India cuts through legal complexity to give you clear, actionable guidance for the situations that actually happen in real life. No jargon. No law degree required.

Inside, you'll learn how to:

File and probate a will, and claim your rightful inheritance

Handle trespassing, nuisance, and neighbor disputes

Enforce your consumer rights and warranty claims

Protect yourself from workplace discrimination and wrongful dismissal

File an FIR — and what to do if the police refuse

Challenge unfair traffic challans

Respond to cybercrime, online fraud, and the new Digital Personal Data Protection Act

Use RTI to demand transparency from government departments

Navigate marriage registration and domestic violence protections

Handle lawyers — how to choose, manage, and if necessary, change them

Inspired by the globally recognized Street Law movement, this book brings that same spirit of legal empowerment to India. Whether you're a student, professional, or first-time litigant, this is the legal companion every Indian household needs.

Read more at https://sivaprasadbose.wordpress.com/.

About the Author

Siva Prasad Bose is an electrical engineer by profession. He is currently retired after many years of service in Uttar Pradesh Power Corporation Limited. He received his engineering degree from Jadavpur University, Kolkata and has a law degree from Meerut University, Meerut. His interests lie in the fields of family law, civil law, law of contracts, and any areas of law related to power electricity related issues.

Read more at https://sivaprasadbose.wordpress.com/.